Four Fars™
at the Park

(An Adventure with Friends who are Different)

By Angel Tucker, CHBC
and
Robert A. Rohm, Ph.D.

Illustrated by Steve Pileggi

Personality
INSIGHTS
PRESS

Series 1 Book 1

Welcome to the "Four Pals"™ Series!

These books were created for three reasons:

1. To show children that they were uniquely created - even our personalities.

2. To teach children all about the different personality types!

3. To let children know that it's okay to feel unique and special as well as be different from their friends!

Here is a further description of each of the personality types. This should assist you in giving your children a better idea of how each of us is different. The important fact to remember is that all children have a unique blend of ALL FOUR of these personality styles. No one will fit neatly into one style. All children will possess some of all of these traits and will exhibit each of the four different types of behavior at different times. Usually, however, one style will emerge as the most predominant trait and this will be the trait the child will demonstrate most often. It will also be the trait that he or she will be most comfortable using on a daily basis. We often say, "That is the way they are wired!"

David

DAVID is our wonderful "**D**" type personality! The letter "**D**" represents the word "**Dominant**." "**D**" type personalities love to be in charge and have things done their own way. "**D**"s think fast and move fast! Their communication style is bottom line oriented. Their attitude is lead, follow, or get out of my way! You never have to wonder what a "**D**" is thinking – they will just tell you! "**D**" children are usually the ones leading all the group activities and telling all the other kids what they will be doing. The "**D**" type personality is **Outgoing and Task-oriented**!

For more great tips on understanding the D-I-S-C child, please get a copy of *A+ Ideas for Every Student's Success* at www.personalityinsights.com or www.personalityprofiles.org

Iris

IRIS is our wonderful "**I**" type personality! The letter "**I**" represents the word "**Inspiring**." "**I**" type personalities love to have fun! They are very optimistic and outgoing! They tend to be forgetful at times because they are usually in a hurry to do things! They like to move fast! Their communication style is exciting and enthusiastic. They don't do well with lots of details and information and may have difficulty accomplishing tasks because they lose their focus. They love being around other people. They thrive on attention and love to entertain others! The "**I**" type personality is **Outgoing and People-oriented**!

Summer

SUMMER is our wonderful "**S**" type personality! The letter "**S**" represents the word "**Supportive**." "**S**" type personalities are very cooperative and pleasant. They do not like conflict. They like peace and harmony. They sometimes have trouble making decisions because they tend to make up their minds slowly. Their communication style is "easy-going." In other words, they tend to adapt easily to whatever is going on around them in their environment. They love people and relationships! "**S**" types love being around other people and helping everyone they meet. They are sensitive and sometimes get their feelings hurt easily. They like to feel appreciated and secure. The "**S**" type personality is **Reserved and People-oriented**!

Charlie

CHARLIE is our wonderful "**C**" type personality! The letter "**C**" represents the word "**Cautious**." "**C**" type personalities enjoy having a routine and schedule. They are usually very good students and like things that challenge their mind. Their communication style is A to Z, which means that details and planning are very important to a "**C**." That is why they ask so many questions. The "**C**" type personality prefers to do things that have been planned out, especially if it involves a large group of people or a lot of activity. They are very comfortable being alone and working independently. They appreciate quality more than quantity. The "**C**" type personality is **Reserved and Task-oriented**!

The "**Four Pals**" series is designed to have 1 book in each series that highlights each of the four different personality styles. There will be 4 more books released in the future.

www.personalityinsights.com or www.personalityprofiles.org

One sunny Saturday, a little boy named David thought it would be an awesome day to go to the park.

David did not want to go to the park alone, so he quickly decided to call some of his friends and tell them to go with him. David loved to be in charge and was sure he could get his friends to go to the park.

The first person he called was his friend Iris. Iris loved to have fun! She squealed with delight when David told her that he wanted her to go to the park. She jumped up and down and said, "This is going to be so exciting!"

"Okay," said David. "Meet me by the big slide at 10 o'clock."
"I'll be there!" Iris replied happily.

Next, David phoned his friend, Summer. He said, "Iris and I are going to the park. Meet us at the big slide at 10 o'clock."

Summer felt so special because they invited her to go to the park also. She loved being with her friends.

Summer noticed that it was 9:00 o'clock and if she hurried, she could bake some cookies for them to eat at the park. Summer loved doing things for others.

Finally, David called his friend, Charlie. He told Charlie that Iris, Summer and he were going to the park and that he should join them. Charlie hesitated and said, "I didn't plan to go to the park today. I usually organize my room and my closet and my toys on Saturdays."

David grunted and said, "Do that later! We're meeting at 10 o'clock by the big slide." Charlie reluctantly agreed and was flustered because he now had to hurry and organize his room.

Before David knew it, it was close to 10 o'clock and he headed to the big slide.

When he arrived at the slide, Summer was already there.
She looked relieved when she saw David.

"I'm so glad you're here! I wasn't sure if I was at the right
slide. I baked us some cookies! Thanks so much for inviting
me!"

Charlie then arrived precisely at 10 o'clock. He had sunscreen for each of them to put on.

David said, "Where's Iris?" Summer was worried that maybe she was lost. Charlie was upset that she wasn't there exactly at 10 o'clock!

About fifteen minutes later, Iris finally arrived. She had a big smile on her face and her hair was in pony tails! "Isn't my hair cute?" she asked. "Guess what! I have a big surprise!"

Not even listening to Iris about her surprise, David scolded, "Where were you? We've been waiting for fifteen minutes!"

"I'm sorry," Iris replied. "I lost track of time." Iris was always losing track of time.

"Well, let's stop wasting time now," exclaimed David.
"Let's go play on the monkey bars." David ran at full speed.
He was determined to be the first one there.

Iris did cartwheels all the way to the monkey bars. "That was fun!" she said.

Summer walked carefully so she wouldn't fall and drop the cookies.

Charlie walked down the sidewalk so he wouldn't get dirt in his shoes. He decided to watch the others on the monkey bars for a little while. He did not want to get blisters on his hands.

After they were finished playing on the monkey bars,
Iris said, "That merry-go-round looks fun! Let's go there
next!" David said, "I want to go to the swings and then
to the slide."

David then told everyone to follow him. He ran quickly towards the swings shouting, "Me first!"

After they finished playing, Summer asked, "Would anyone like some cookies?"

"Yeah!" said David, "I want the biggest one."

Iris was having great fun with her cookie! She was breaking it into pieces and popping them into her mouth!

Charlie said, "I am going to wash my hands before I eat my cookie," and he headed off to the restroom.

Summer made sure everyone else had enough cookies before she ate any.

After they finished their cookies, David said, "It's time to go. I need to get home now."

"Thanks again for inviting me," said Summer. "I had a wonderful time."

"Me too!" Iris said. "Friends are fun!"

Then Charlie said, "Iris, I believe there was something you wanted to tell us earlier. What was it?"

"Oh yeah," said Iris. "I almost forgot! My mom said she would take us to the zoo next Saturday. Can all of you come?"

Each of her friends said they would be able
to come as long as their mom or dad said it was okay.
This made Iris incredibly happy and she jumped up
and down. Iris loved the idea of everyone going to
the zoo together! Iris said, "Awesome! Now I have
one more thing to look forward to."

"Yeah, me too!" each of her friends replied. And they all went home glad that even though they were all very different, they could still be great friends and have great adventures together.

Reader's Guide

This is Book 1 in this series. The focus in this book is on David – the **Dominant** "D" type personality! To get all four books in the "Four Pals" series go to the website: www.personalityinsights.com or www.personalityprofiles.org or call 1-800-509-DISC (3472)

The focus in this book is on David

David

Did you notice in this story how David likes to be in charge? He doesn't seem to consider the fact that at times, he might be coming across a little "bossy" to his friends. He is a natural born "take charge" kind of person. This personality style is often looked at as a natural born leader. If he uses this trait in the right way, he will grow up to become an outstanding leader who will influence many, many people.

Iris

Did you observe in this story how Iris likes to have fun and play? She occasionally does not pay close enough attention to detail and appears to be "unfocused" at times. But, everyone loves her because of her happy nature! She is a natural born talker and a very energetic kind of person. She is always helping everyone around her to have fun. If she uses this trait in the right way she will always help other people to feel happy and laugh a lot!

Charlie

Did you notice in this story how Charlie liked to have everything in order in his life? Charlie believes it is important to obey the rules and to do things right! Sometimes Charlie is very serious, but he is working on having a little more fun. He is an excellent student and does well in school. Charlie may enjoy becoming a physician, a pilot, an accountant, a lawyer, or a scientist. If he uses his traits in the right way, he will grow up to be very successful in whatever area he studies!

Summer

Did it warm your heart to watch the way Summer helped all of her friends? She was thoughtful and cared about what other people might want. She consistently put her friends ahead of herself, which is a good thing to do. She is also learning that she is important and has needs, too! If she uses her traits in the right way, she will make a lot of people feel special. When you hear someone say, "Have a nice day," they are really saying, "I hope you meet a lot of people like Summer" or "I hope you act like Summer today and are kind and gentle towards everyone you meet!"

"Four Pals"
and the Model of Human Behavior

Each of us has an internal "motor" that drives us. It has a fast pace that makes us more **Outgoing**, or it has a slower pace that makes us more **Reserved**. You may be extremely **Outgoing** or **Reserved**, or you may be just be moderately **Outgoing** or **Reserved**. In either case, your "internal motor" creates a certain pace about you that drives you to do your daily activities at a certain rate of speed. Knowing how you are "wired" will help you to monitor yourself in life so you will either go faster or slower depending upon the requirements or needs of the existing environment.

OUTGOING

Internal "Motor" Activity

RESERVED

Just as we have a motor that drives us, we also have a "compass" that draws us toward either task or people. Therefore, we are either **Task-oriented** or **People-oriented**. You may find yourself to be extremely **Task-oriented** or **People-oriented**, or you may be just be moderately **Task-oriented** or **People-oriented**. In either case, your "internal compass" creates a certain direction about you that drives you to do your daily activities in a certain manner that either reflects your desire to accomplish daily tasks or connect well with people. Knowing how you are "wired" will help you to monitor yourself in life so you will either focus on the task at hand or seek to relate well with the people with whom you come in contact on a daily basis, depending upon the requirements or needs of the existing environment.

T A S K

Internal "Compass" Activity

P E O P L E

When we put together both the Internal "Motor" Activity and the Internal "Compass" Activity, we see the four quadrant DISC **Model of Human Behavior**. Illustrated below we see in clockwise order that:

The D type is
Outgoing / Task-oriented

The I type is
Outgoing / People-oriented

David
The Dominant Type

Iris
The Inspiring Type

Charlie
The Cautious Type

Summer
The Supportive Type

OUTGOING & TASK

OUTGOING & PEOPLE

RESERVED & TASK

RESERVED & PEOPLE

D I C S

The C type is
Reserved / Task-oriented

The S type is
Reserved / People-oriented

Introducing the Dominant type child

Key Characteristics

Dominant
Direct
Demanding
Decisive
Determined
Doer

- has a strong ego
- dares to be different
- is not afraid to take risks
- likes to be in control
- is goal-oriented
- likes new and varied activities
- loves to compete and win
- is a self-starter

Value to the Family or their Group

- works for result
- speaks out openly
- loves adventure
- a natural leader
- is good at organizing events
- takes leadership position
- likes to solve problems
- acts quickly and independently

The D Danger Zone

- may be argumentative
- oversteps authority
- is bored with routine
- can be pushy or impatient
- may be belligerent
- may ignore the rules to succeed

The D Type Child Says:

As a High D child, I often make plans because I like to make things happen. I want to show you that I can do things myself. I love to take charge of myself and others. When I work, I work hard; when I play, I play hard. I will try almost anything if I think it will work. I like to make decisions and I don't like doing the same old things all the time, so I question the way things are done. I can be demanding when I think that I have a better way, or if I feel that your decision may not be in my best interest. I tell you what I think and I get straight to the point. Oftentimes, I do not realize that I may make you feel challenged. I am not trying to do that. I just like knowing who is in control. I need to learn that in order to be in authority I must first learn to be under authority. This is a challenge for me! I am full of energy and want to do great things with my life!

Keys to the heart of your Dominant child

Communication Key – your D Child says:

- tell me what you want me to do
- show me what I can accomplish
- be direct and clear
- offer me choices if you can let me decide about something

Encouragement Key – say to your D Child:

- "You are confident and quick to respond."
- "I like that you tell me exactly what you think!"
- "You can see a problem and figure out a way to solve it."
- "When you want to do something important, sometimes we can work together!"

Parenting Keys for your Dominant Child:

As you parent a D type child, you will feel the strength of their drive. This is a wonderful strength that will allow them to accomplish many great things where others may give up. As a parent you need to help your child keep this strength under control. Out of control, this drive may make them argue with anything you ask them to do. This is so very trying for you! What they really need is to learn that you mean what you say. Take the time to explain situations to them, then give them choices so they can better cooperate with you to do what you ask. Teaching them to accept limits, even when they disagree with you, prepares them for the realities of life.

The High D child often appears to be angry when things don't go as planned, or when someone else chooses the plan. Try to remember that this anger is actually fear of losing control. Until they mature and understand their powerful personality style, it may often be beyond their control. Allow the D child as many choices as you can, but do not allow them to take control away from you. When you do, you will struggle to regain the control you need. Their anger will always hinder them unless they learn to use it constructively. They need to understand that failure is an event that happens, not a person. This child is amazing!

About the Authors

Angel Tucker is a wife, mom and national speaker/trainer. As a Certified Human Behavior Consultant and owner of Personality Profiles, LLC, she has been speaking and training professionally across North America for the past 23 years. She began by teaching churches and youth groups. She instantly knew it was her desire to share this life changing information with as many people as possible. Angel and her husband Dennis, who is an officer in the United States Air Force, have five children – Danielle, Chase, Hannah, Elijah and Ava. When Dennis retires, they plan to travel the country together – teaching and training others about our wonderful personalities!

If you are interested in having Angel speak at your next engagement, please contact her using the following information:

Website: www.personalityprofiles.org
Email: personalitypro@msn.com

Dr. Robert A. Rohm is a renowned National and International speaker. He has traveled all over the world including every continent (except Antarctica), teaching and training people in the D-I-S-C Model of Human Behavior. Most people consider Dr. Rohm to be one of the leading authorities in the world on understanding personality styles and relationship dynamics.

Dr. Rohm has been an educator for over 40 years. He has earned 5 college degrees and has written or co-authored over 20 books as well as writing over 600 published articles. He also has numerous audio and video training programs including two PBS Specials.

Dr. Rohm is a husband, father and grandfather and believes that those roles have been the true source for many of his insights and learning experiences. He has entertained and enlightened audiences for many years. His mixture of stories, illustrations, and humor make him a gifted speaker to audiences of all ages!

Dr. Rohm is also the co-founder of discoveryreport.com

To learn more about Dr. Robert Rohm or have him at your event, go to: www.robertrohm.com or www.personalityinsights.com or call Personality Insights, Inc. at (800) 509-DISC (3472).

Discover more...

Here is one of the most accurate tools available for DISCovering children's personality styles. Purpose: To help parents, teachers and individuals who work with children better understand them, and for the children to understand themselves and others by explaining tendencies. This resource material provides insights on tendencies as your child develops and matures. Additional insights are approaching instructions, motivational tips, and pointers on ideal environment and communication.

Children's Version (Ages 5-12)

This one-of-a-kind assessment is designed specifically for children. It is a fun and interactive way for parents and teachers to gain insights into individual preferences or choices the child makes based on robot characters (BOTS).

The stories allow children as young as 5 years old to complete the assessment.

www.personalityinsights.com

www.personalityprofiles.org

www.discoveryreport.com